This book belongs to:

....

The author and publisher are indebted to James McCracken, B.D.S.
(University of Glasgow) and Diane Melvin, child psychologist, for their
invaluable help in the preparation of this book.

First published in 1989 by Conran Octopus Limited
This edition published in 2002 by Brimax,
an imprint of Octopus Publishing Group Ltd
2-4 Heron Quays, London E14 4JP

A CIP catalogue record for this book is available from the British Library.

ISBN 1 85854 565 X

Printed in China

First Experiences

Danny Goes to the Dentist

Written by **Robert Robinson**
Illustrated by **Nicola Smee**

BRIMAX

It's almost time for bed. Mother is reading Danny and Vicki a book all about teeth. Tomorrow, they are going to visit the dentist.

The dentist isn't far from their home.
Danny and Vicki play all the way there.

DENTIST

"We've come for a check up," says Mother,
and tells the receptionist their names.
The receptionist finds their record cards.

The waiting room is full of people. Danny sees his friend, Matthew. They play cars together while they wait. Mother reads Vicki a story.

Soon the nurse comes to take them to the dentist's room. Mother comes with them.

"Hello, you two," says the dentist. "How are you?"
"I've lost my first baby tooth," says Danny, proudly.
"You'll lose more as you get older," says the dentist,
"and get new ones in their place."

"Now then, who wants to be first?" he asks.
"Me please," says Vicki, quickly climbing on
to the chair.

The nurse ties a bib around Vicki's neck
to stop her clothes from getting wet.

"I like this chair," says Vicki. "Can I make it go up and down like I did last time?"
"Of course," laughs the dentist.
Vicki pushes a button and the chair goes back.

"How are your teeth?" asks the dentist.
"They are fine, thank you," says Vicki.
"Let's have a look," says the dentist.
"Open wide."

The dentist gently checks Vicki's teeth with a thin, pointed instrument. He uses a little mirror on a stick to see the top ones.

"They seem fine," says the dentist. "Now I'll give them a polish to make them extra clean."
Vicki likes having her teeth polished. The brush tickles and the paste tastes of mint.

"Your turn now, Danny," says the dentist.
"I want to see your new tooth."
Danny gets on to the chair and opens his
mouth wide.

The dentist looks at all Danny's teeth.
He tells the nurse what he sees and she makes
notes on Danny's card.
"Don't forget his new tooth," says Vicki.

The dentist finds a hole in one of Danny's teeth.
"I think that you have been eating too many
sweet things," he says. "I am going to clean out
the tooth a little with my drill and put in
a filling for you."

The drill makes a rumbling noise but it doesn't hurt Danny very much.

The nurse makes a filling mixture which looks like white toothpaste. The dentist fills Danny's tooth with it. "Leave your mouth open for a minute while this hardens," he says.

When the tooth is ready, Danny takes a sip of mouthwash. He swishes it around his mouth and spits into a funnel.

"All done," says the dentist. "Now remember to take good care of your teeth. I want you to brush them twice a day and try not to eat too many sweets."
He gives them both a balloon and a poster.

On the way out, the receptionist lets Vicki and Danny choose a sticker each. Mother buys them both a new toothbrush.

At bedtime, they use their toothbrushes. They clean their teeth really well and remove every bit of food.

Mother puts up the poster in their room.
"If I eat what this says, I hope I won't ever
need another filling," says Danny.

Eat these for
treats not
sticky sweets